S0-BQZ-356

A Beginning-to-Read Book

Who Goes to School?

by Margaret Hillert

Illustrated by Nan Brooks

NORWOOD HOUSE PRESS

DEAR CAREGIVER,

The *Beginning-to-Read* series is a carefully written collection of classic readers you may remember from your own childhood. Each book features text comprised of common sight words to provide your child ample practice reading the words that appear most frequently in written text. The many additional details in the pictures enhance the story and offer the opportunity for you to help your child expand oral language and develop comprehension.

Begin by reading the story to your child, followed by letting him or her read familiar words and soon your child will be able to read the story independently. At each step of the way, be sure to praise your reader's efforts to build his or her confidence as an independent reader. Discuss the pictures and encourage your child to make connections between the story and his or her own life. At the end of the story, you will find reading activities and a word list that will help your child practice and strengthen beginning reading skills.

Above all, the most important part of the reading experience is to have fun and enjoy it!

Shannon Cannon

Shannon Cannon,
Literacy Consultant

Norwood House Press • P.O. Box 316598 • Chicago, Illinois 60631
For more information about Norwood House Press please visit our website at *www.norwoodhousepress.com* or call 866-565-2900.

LIBRARY OF CONGRESS CATALOGING-IN-PUBLICATION DATA

Hillert, Margaret.
  Who goes to school? / by Margaret Hillert ; illustrated by Nan Brooks.—
Rev. and expanded library ed.
     p. cm.— (Beginning to read series. Easy stories)
  Summary: Simple text and illustrations depict animals in various work and training situations and concludes that school can be fun for animals and children. Includes reading activities.
  ISBN-13: 978-1-59953-032-1 (library edition : alk. paper)
  ISBN-10: 1-59953-032-5 (library edition : alk. paper)
  [1. Animals—Training—Fiction. 2. Working animals—Fiction. 3. Schools—Fiction. 4. Readers.] I. Brooks, Nan, ill. II. Title. III. Series.
  PZ7.H558Wh 2006
  [E]—dc22   2005033535

Who goes to school?
Can you guess?
No, no.
You can not guess,
but you will see.

Look here.
Look at this.
This is a school.
A school for dogs.

The dog will sit.
The dog will walk.
The dog will go with you.
This is good.

Here is a school, too.
And here are big dogs.
See what the big dogs do.

This dog gets into a car.
This dog will work.
He will work with the man.

Here is a good dog.
See this dog work.
He is a big help.

The dog will go out.
He will look and look.
He will find something.

See this dog.
What can he do?
What is he good for?

This dog can work.
He can do good work.
He can help the man see.

And look at this little one.
What can he do?
Oh, look at this.

He did it!
He did it!
He is good.
What fun this is.

Here is a big baby.
It can do something, too.

It can sit up.

And here are big cats.
Big, big cats.

Cats at school.

The big cats sit.
The big cats play.
We like to see this.

Little cats go to school, too.
Look at this cat.
What a pretty one.

Now look at the TV.
Here is the little cat.
See what work she can do.
She is on TV.

This cat gets something.

She gets something little.
She is a big help.

This cat helps, too.
The man likes the cat.
What a good little cat.

Here is a school.
Boys and girls go to
this school.

Do you go to school, too?

Yes, you do.
You read.
You work.
You play, too.

You have fun here.
It is fun to go to school.

READING REINFORCEMENT

The following activities support the findings of the National Reading Panel that determined the most effective components for reading instruction are: Phonemic Awareness, Phonics, Vocabulary, Fluency, and Text Comprehension.

Phonemic Awareness: The /w/ Sound

Sound Substitution: Say the words on the left to your child. Ask your child to repeat the word, changing the first sound to /w/:

talk = walk	me = we	pill = will	pay = way
mall= wall	cake = wake	save = wave	tag = wag
bear = wear	pin = win	dish = wish	poke = woke
nest = west	need = weed	paste = waste	bait = wait

Phonics: The letter Ww

1. Demonstrate how to form the letters **W** and **w** for your child.
2. Have your child practice writing **W** and **w** at least three times each.
3. Ask your child to point to the words in the book that start with the letter **w**.
4. Write down the following words and ask your child to circle the letter **w** in each word:

we	who	work	paw	with	cow	crawl
well	will	throw	what	walk	tower	low

Vocabulary: Animal Sounds

1. Write the following words on separate pieces of sticky note paper:

cat	dog	lion	bee	duck	bird	donkey
sheep	owl	chirp	roar	baa	hee haw	hoo
meow	quack	woof	buzz			

2. Read each word for your child.

3. Mix up the words and ask your child to match the animal names with the correct sound.

4. Mix up the words again and say each word randomly. Ask your child to point to the correct word as you say it.

Fluency: Echo Reading

1. Reread the story to your child at least two more times while your child tracks the print by running a finger under the words as they are read. Ask your child to read the words he or she knows with you.

2. Reread the story, stopping after each sentence or page to allow your child to read (echo) what you have read. Repeat echo reading and let your child take the lead.

Text Comprehension: Discussion Time

1. Ask your child to retell the sequence of events in the story.

2. To check comprehension, ask your child the following questions:

   - How did the cat help people in the story?

   - What was the elephant trained to do in the story?

   - Why do you think dogs can help find people in the snow?

   - What did the kids do at school?

   - Do you have a pet?

     - If so, what have you trained it to do?

     - If not, what kind of pet would you like to have? What would you train it to do?

WORD LIST

Who Goes to School? uses the 65 words listed below.

This list can be used to practice reading the words that appear in the text. You may wish to write the words on index cards and use them to help your child build automatic word recognition. Regular practice with these words will enhance your child's fluency in reading connected text.

a	find	in	oh	the
and	for	into	on	this
are	fun	is	one	to
at		it	out	too
	gets			TV
baby	girls	like (s)	play	
big	go	little	pretty	up
boys	goes	look		
but	good		read	walk
	guess	man		we
can			school	what
car	have	no	see	who
cat (s)	he	not	she	will
	help (s)	now	sit	with
did	here		something	work
do				
dog (s)				yes
				you

ABOUT THE AUTHOR Margaret Hillert has written over 80 books for children who are just learning to read. Her books have been translated into many different languages and over a million children throughout the world have read her books. She first started writing poetry as a child and has continued to write for children and adults throughout her life. A first grade teacher for 34 years, Margaret is now retired from teaching and lives in Michigan where she likes to write, take walks in the morning, and care for her three cats.

Photograph by Glenna Washburn

ABOUT THE ADVISER Shannon Cannon contributed the activities pages that appear in this book. Shannon serves as a literacy consultant and provides staff development to help improve reading instruction. She is a frequent presenter at educational conferences and workshops. Prior to this she worked as an elementary school teacher and as president of a curriculum publishing company.